PLATFORMS

– encounters by the railside

Bob Sheed

Bob Sheed was born in Derbyshire and has lived in South Yorkshire, East Anglia, London and Rotterdam. He now lives in Teddington with his wife Tricia.

By the same author

The Wild Bunch – Poems for the Unruly
So What Do We Do Now? – 30 Tales of Perplexity
Dragon's Breath and Other Stories (editor)
Games and Promises – Poems for the Reckless
No, I Think I'll Leave It – Familiar Tales Re-told in Rhyme

For Gabby, Laura, Millie and Nicole

PLATFORMS

Two long carriages and thirteen short ones carry stories of lives changed through events acted out on a station platform.

CONTENTS

La Femme du train

I don't know about you, but personally I don't much look for
answers. Things happen, and when they do, 'that's life,' I
say. So when a woman got on the train this morning and sat
down in the seat opposite, I wasn't going to say anything
about the cow's head on a pole that she was carrying. I was
getting off soon anyway (at Ely). The most I would have to
endure, I thought, would be the inane small talk that
passengers boarding at Thetford sometimes engage you in.

Though I tried hard, it was difficult not to look at her.
She was wearing a straw boater with some writing on the
hat band and I couldn't help flicking a glance or two at it.
She twice caught my eye and although each time I
immediately steered my gaze away, she eventually leaned
forward and tapped me on the knee.

'Do you mind keeping an eye on this little lady for a
minute?' she said. 'I'm dying for a shit.'

'You'd better be quick,' I said, 'I'm getting off at Ely,'
but she was half-way up the carriage by then and she called
back something that I didn't catch, but I suspect it was of a
scatological nature because a girl of about eight gave a
squeal and her mother shot her a dirty look.

At some point in these proceedings I seem to have
taken hold of the pole. A cow's eyes now stared into mine
and the expression on its face was that same mixture of
amusement and incredulity that you will have seen on the
face of Jeremy Paxman when a politician gives him an
unsatisfactory answer.

I stared back. It was, I could now see, rather too small
for a cow's head – a *real* cow's head, I mean – although apart
from that it was exceptionally lifelike. Gingerly, because

those eyes were quite unnerving, I stroked the skin. I'd expected it to have a felt-like texture, but it wasn't like that at all. It was like touching the skin of a cow. I rubbed its ears and they were sort of, well, it's difficult to find the right word: gristly, I suppose you might say; not floppy at all. With an increasing sense of horror, I put my hand to my own ear and it had the same springy quality. Oh my God! It *is* a cow's head! It even had one of those identity tags on its ear.

Now, given half a chance, I would have propped the creature against the window and slunk away, but the train had just stopped at Brandon and a young Asian woman with a Sri Lankan Airlines shoulder bag and an iPod in her ear had sat down opposite me in the seat next to the window. A look of outrage sprang to her face as she saw what I was holding, although if you ask me she had less to grumble about than I did, religious sensibilities notwithstanding, not having to face that disbelieving stare. The woman's eyes darted around the carriage, as though tracking a fly, but there was no other seat she could easily move to, and by now I had slid the foot of the pole across the floor to block her exit. Why should I suffer this alone, eh?

A few tense moments followed in which I was happy to withdraw into a staring match with the child who had squealed earlier. Then the door to the toilet compartment slid open (or rather half open, there being a case partially blocking the way) and the owner of the bovine device barged clumsily through. She gave the Indian woman an affronted look, then plonked herself down in the seat next to her. She leaned towards me and said, 'no bloody toilet paper and no soap.' Then she beckoned me forward and whispered in my ear, 'I thought I told you to keep that seat for me.'

I began to protest, but she waved a hand in front of me and started coughing.

'That's *"Pour Homme"*, isn't it?' she said when she'd got her breath back. 'I'm allergic to Yves St Laurent.'

I did not feel inclined to apologise for my choice of after-shave, and I told her so.

'All right. All right. Just keep away from me, that's all.' I confirmed that I would have no trouble in doing this, and I took the opportunity of thrusting the pole with the cow's head back into her possession.

'Careful!' said the woman. 'She's a Royal you know.'

'What?'

'Ségolène. That's what the man called her. You remember, Ségolène Royal? One time French socialist presidential candidate? Not everybody's friend, obviously. I bought her last week at a French farmers' market in Cambridge. Look, the name's printed on her *"boucle d'oreille"*.' Her accent bore the unmistakable sing-song of French as it is spoken in Ipswich. She twisted the identity tag around for me to read.

'What you might call a "socialist sacred cow",' I said, trying to be clever.

The woman tipped her boater. 'Nice one, sunshine. She's a hobby-horse; a hobby-calf really.'

Of course! I thought: not a cow, a calf; that's why it's so small!

'Nicely embalmed, or freeze-dried, I'm not sure. My French didn't stretch that far. I'm in an all-female Morris side. You know, Morris dancing?' She pointed to the writing on her hat band which I could now see read: "Mildenhall Morris Maids".

'We've been everywhere: Sri Lanka, Egypt. Lost our last hobby-horse in a riot in Notting Hill.'

We can't be far from Ely now, I thought. I took a look at the electronic sign at the end of the carriage. Red letters were skating across the LCD display. 'This is Norwich,' it

3

read deceptively. 'This train terminates here. Please take all your belongings with you.'

'I know,' said my companion, following my eye. 'Sodding typical.'

As Ely Cathedral swam into sight, the train began to slow and I stood up and swung around. This left me facing away from the nearest door and down the carriage to the door at the far end, but it meant I could avoid eye contact with the calf and its owner. When the doors opened I leapt out, in what for a delicious moment felt like a bound for freedom. I was that figure in the old newsreel, dropping from the Berlin Wall into no-man's-land! Ah, those precious seconds of euphoria before the bullet ripped into my body.

'Sorry!'

I took a sideways jump as the pair stepped out in front of me – from the other door, obviously. 'That was a bit rude of me.'

'Um?' I said.

'Complaining about your after-shave. It's only a problem in a confined space. Out here on the platform it's perfectly fine,' she concluded, as she slipped her arm through mine and fell into step beside me.

Ariadne

'Have you been to Ragusa?'

The young woman took off her hat as she spoke and I suffered a moment of panic as I struggled to connect the question with the gesture. Pretty women always put me in a tizzy, unsettling me by their beauty and, in my confusion, causing me to say something ridiculous. I can't recall now whether I said anything at all in reply. I probably didn't because almost at once she went on. 'The colours don't do it justice, of course.' She swept her hand in the direction of a poster on the tube station wall, obliging a young man who had been standing in front of it to step awkwardly to one side. He shot an accusing look at me, as though it had been I, and not the woman, who had come close to striking him.

Until that moment I hadn't registered the existence of the poster. I saw now that it was a picture of the Sicilian town of Ragusa: an advertisement for a film about some exploit of Inspector Montalbano, the Sicilian detective of television fame.

'Not as good as the book,' I said, repeating the comments of a film critic I'd just been reading in that day's "Metro". I regretted it immediately.

The woman said something in Italian which, from the bit of Latin I'd picked up at school, I guessed meant 'have you read it?' I said I hadn't.

'Then you can't know that, can you?' Her eyes, startlingly blue, locked on to mine.

'No. I suppose not,' I said, ready to lie down on the platform and let her stamp on my face.

'Anyway, that isn't the point. I was talking about the place.' The rumble of an approaching train raised a stir among the waiting commuters and a fierce rush of air swept along the platform. Absurdly, neither of us turned around or paid it any attention.

When the train had gone, she said, 'I need to go there one last time: to Ragusa.' I looked sideways at her and it was then, and only then, I swear, that I noticed she was completely bald. 'I've told them to stop the treatment.' She smiled. 'You'll come with me, won't you?' My tongue refused to leave the roof of my mouth and my arms seemed to be bound to my sides. I suppose I must have nodded because how else would I have come to be in Ragusa today? 'My name is Ariadne' she said. 'If you've read Chekhov, that will not surprise you.'

Bina and the Boy

Bina scrambles inelegantly from the car.

'God is great,' says her brother.

Bina repeats the words, but her eyes have broken from his before she has uttered the final syllable.

Now she is picking her way along the hot, dusty path. It is unevenly paved and has not been swept for days. Her small body is clothed in the blue and gold shalwar kameez she wore to her sister's wedding, little more than a month ago. Meera, certainly pregnant by now, had pressed a cold hand into hers as she was led away by her eager, and not unhandsome, new husband.

Bina now wishes she had chosen more sensible shoes, as she steps fearfully on the troublesome flagstones. Her thickened waist, to which she is still not accustomed, makes her tottering progress even more unsteady.

The heels thrust her forward, yet she must lean back to balance the weight she carries before her. She moves a hand to her tummy, running her fingertips uncertainly over her new shape.

What sacrifices women make for the sake of the next generation, she ponders – men too, of course. Luckily she does not have far to go, and the tiny paces she is obliged to take will soon cover the ground.

She has reached the railway station. A ticket inspector takes hold of her ticket, barely looking at it, his eyes moving instead to her tummy. Bina flushes and the inspector smiles. Pregnancy and first-class tickets clearly touch his heart. He clips the ticket and she passes through the barrier.

As she makes her way to the end of the platform where she knows the first-class carriage will stop, a beggar springs up in her path. He is ragged and barely pubescent. The trail of a tear traces the contours of his small, pinched face and there is a fresh cut on his arm. Bina attempts a sidestep, almost colliding with him, as she tries to manoeuvre her way around. The boy is nimble, however, and used to dodges of this kind. Immediately, he is again in front of her.

'Please let me pass', she implores. 'I am on God's business.'

Her pleadings get her nowhere. Hopping from foot to foot, the urchin continues to thrust out a hand, saying nothing. It is not to make conversation that he has scrambled through the barbed-wire fence.

Bina's eye is caught by the swirl of a white sari some ten metres away. A tall woman, her high forehead sweating in the late morning sun, is being hurried to the First-Class waiting room. Bina, urged by the demands of Destiny, forces a way past the shimmying bundle of rags. But Destiny has other plans. As Bina stumbles towards the Indian ambassador, the ragamuffin makes a grab for the hem of her kameez, sending her reeling to the ground and detonating prematurely the five kilogrammes of Semtex she has strapped around her middle.

Chattanooga

I have to be careful; there are cameras about.

I was engaged to play the part of a shoe-shine boy, but they needed someone to sweep the platform before they could start shooting and because I am not a real actor, the director stuck a broom in my hand and told me to get rid of the leaves.

A sign says 'Welcome to Chattanooga', although this is actually Shippea Hill, a little-used station on the edge of the Cambridgeshire fens. We are, as you might guess, working on a shoestring. This is how I got the part, despite not being a professional performer. Even so, they are lucky to get me. I have at least done a bit of acting at my old school in Ely. I can do a fair impression of a southern states African-American boy, saying 'Yes Massa!' while rolling my eyes. The script relies heavily on stereotypes that are not very popular nowadays. The director claims the film is an ironical interpretation. The fact that I am as white as a celery root is apparently part of the irony, although this is not something we sons of the soil can be expected to understand.

Anyway, as I said, I have to be careful. In the process of sweeping the leaves, I have uncovered something: a broach by the look of it. Rays from the early afternoon sun are bouncing off stones that must surely be diamonds.

I am as honest, and as deceitful, as any fen-blown* boy. That is to say, the path I ought to take is often occluded by clouds whipped up by forces outside my control. There is absolutely no reason why I should not pick up the object and hand it to someone in authority. The trouble is, the only authority around right now is the director, a man whose eyes are set closer together than they would be on the face of an honest man. The railway operators do not maintain any staff at this station, which sees a passenger only once or twice a month.

I sweep some leaves over the item in question and consider the position. Whoever lost the piece must be long gone. They've had plenty of time to come back for it, because it's late autumn now and the leaves have been off the trees for weeks. 'Finders, keepers' has never seemed a more appropriate dictum. And yet, as I said, I must be careful; there are cameras about.

Cameras. Ah yes! Cameras! Suddenly, like an actor playing St Paul on the road to Damascus, I am hit by a blinding light: the only trees growing by Shippea Hill station are a few miserable poplars. The leaves I am sweeping are from a maple. Trust me, bro'. I am your country cousin.

Someone has planted the leaves here, pun and irony joined in sin. But to what end? And if the leaves are here by human hand then might not the broach, if that's what it is, also be a plant?

I lean my broom against the fence and look around. I can't see a camera but I know there must be one. Perhaps they're filming from that building across the road, or maybe from the signal box. 'Come out, come out wherever you are!' I call.

In a moment the director appears. Far from being congratulated on my perspicacity, I am accused of ruining the shot. 'I needed the shoe-shine boy to steal that broach,' he says. 'The only way I could get you to do it was if you did it for real. I knew you couldn't act the part, you peat-brained dummy!'

'Well, ain't this a swell party!' I said. 'But since you're such a nice guy, I'll save your day and act out the scene.'

And that is just what I did. Perfectly.

The Elephant Man

It was the string of elephants hanging in a garland around his neck that caught Brenda's attention: eight small straw figures, each one decorated with a different coloured ribbon looped under its chin and gathered on top of its head in a bow. The man was wearing a long, off-white shirt which hung down to below his knees, over baggy trousers of the same material. The word 'calico' came into Brenda's mind, though she wasn't quite sure what kind of material calico was. Would an Indian man be wearing calico? Brenda was sure he must be Indian. His colouring, his black hair and the string of elephants couldn't mean anything else. She looked at his hands, long fingers interlocking across his stomach. He had a straw bag hanging from one arm.

'Hello,' she said. The man looked around him. He was tall, even taller than most people seemed to Brenda. At four feet ten, she was used to being missed in the crowd. She gave a little wave. 'Down here!'

'Ah yes,' said the man. He smiled, but did not seem ready to say anything more.

'The elephants,' said Brenda. 'Very unusual.' She pointed. 'They're very pretty.' The man looked down. For a moment he appeared surprised to see them.

'Ah yes,' he said again, but this time, since Brenda continued to stare at him, he evidently felt the need to add something. 'I sell them.' He jiggled the bag on his arm, but did not offer to open it.

'How much?'

'I'm sorry?' The man bent towards her, and Brenda caught the smell of some rather pleasant aftershave as his head came closer to hers.

'How much do you charge? I might decide to buy one.'

The man straightened up. 'There I cannot help you, madam. I am not allowed to trade on the station platform.'

That might have been the end of the matter. A train pulled into the station and Brenda got into a first class carriage. The man headed in the other direction. She refused to allow herself to think it was only natural that he would be travelling standard class.

They met again a week later. The doorbell rang and when she opened the front door, there he stood. He was wearing the same elephant garland and he had more draped over his arm. He smiled, but it was clear he did not recognise her.

'I'm sorry,' she said. 'I don't buy at the door.'

Flood

It came about after the seven days, that the water of the flood came upon the earth – *Genesis 6:10*

A week after they carted Harry off in a police van, the water poured into the valley. Inch by inch, houses, shops, school and railway station slipped below the surface. A torrent at first, as the level reached the first storeys of the buildings, the flood calmed, so that the water rippled and swirled rather than thrashed and thundered. It was as though a great lake were being filled from below, which indeed it was.

Never destined for great things, Harry had spent fifty years in the employ of the company operating the national rail network – the last forty in charge of the local station. When a new motorway passed within a mile of the village, the branch line closed and Harry was out of a job. The company let him stay on at the station-master's house which he had occupied for forty years, in exchange for which he kept the platforms swept and weeded. The company hadn't yet decided what to do with the land and it seemed sensible to have the place kept tidy while they thought about it.

After a while men came with surveying equipment and took measurements. Fearful of what this activity might portend, Harry asked no questions. When letters arrived telling him the land on which the house and former station stood had been sold to a water company, he ran his eyes over them but the information they contained refused to lodge in his head. When the time came to put out the rubbish, the letters went in the bin.

Eventually, after several visits to his home had failed to shift him, the bailiffs came with a police escort and he was taken to his widowed sister's house a few miles away. She was no more pleased than he was at the turn of events. When a few months later the council found him a sheltered accommodation flat back in his old village, they parted no closer in sibling affection than they had been since the day she tried to smother him in his cot.

Almost a year had passed since his eviction and although social services had him on their books, nobody thought he would attempt to return to his old home. After all, it was under twenty feet of water in the middle of the new reservoir.

The water was dark but he had a torch and in the depths of the still water he found he could swim quite comfortably. He located the old platform, some unfamiliar grasses growing through cracks and shoals of brightly-coloured fish swimming in and out of an upstairs window of his old house. It was too small for him to swim through and when he went in search of the front door it didn't seem to be in the right place. I'm disorientated, he thought, swimming around to the back, but when he found a door, it was locked. How foolish not to have brought the key!

He swam away, keeping close to the edge of the platform till he came to the spot where he'd once grabbed a man's coat as he was about to jump in front of a train. An image of his face in the local newspaper – 'Railway Hero' – drifted in front of him. Further on he found some twisted rails. A train had come off the track here but only because he'd diverted it by jamming some wrongly set points to prevent it colliding with one coming the other way. He was surprised that after all those years the rails hadn't been replaced.

He discovered other places, where other memories came flooding back: the shabbily-dressed woman who'd had her purse stolen, along with the ticket she needed to visit her son in prison. He'd bought her another out of his own pocket. When she returned a month later to repay him, he suspected she'd gone without food in order to get the money together. He told her it wasn't necessary, but pride is important to those who have little else to sustain them and he finally accepted it with thanks.

Not a bad life, he thought.

Deaths are not uncommon in sheltered accommodation. Wardens count themselves lucky if a winter goes by without finding at least one elderly resident dead in their beds.

'Here's an odd one,' said the pathologist to his assistant. 'Apart from no evidence of water in the lungs, I'd have sworn from the other symptoms that this one drowned.'

The Woman on the Bicycle

I might not have noticed her at all if she hadn't wheeled her bike into me. 'Christ!' I shouted, more out of surprise than anything, as the front wheel went over my foot, but when the pedal hit my ankle I came out with something stronger because *that* really hurt.

'I'm sorry,' she said, in a distracted sort of way, not actually looking at me. Then she asked if the next train to Hampton Court had places for bicycles.

'How the hell would I know?' I said, not realising she wasn't talking to me. A man in a uniform – possibly a railway employee – told her she would have to fold it up.

'But it's not a folding one,' she wailed, in a voice so plaintive that I actually felt sorry for her when the man walked away. Whether I would have acted upon this unexpected burst of sympathy, it's impossible to say, if I hadn't become suddenly intrigued by the realisation that I had seen her before.

'Don't bother about him,' I said. 'Just wheel it on. I've never heard anyone complain.' She gave a wan smile but when I told her I felt sure I knew her from somewhere, the smile turned languidly into a frown. 'Look, I'm not trying to chat you up,' I said. I would have gone on but it was clear that here was someone who did not do her thinking in the fast lane. The frown melted slowly, like ice giving way in a gin and tonic, to be followed by a look of mild puzzlement.

She drew her brows together as if in thought but the effort seemed too much for her. She leaned the bicycle against a post and, seeming not to know what to do with her hands, put one to her chin.

I asked her if she'd been to any parties in the last month or so. I was sure I'd seen her recently. She shook her head and I had to admit that she wasn't the kind of person anyone I knew would be likely to invite to a party. Then quite suddenly she took hold of my elbow.

'I'm sorry about your foot.'

'That's all right,' I said, taking her hand and lifting it from my arm. I bent down to rub my ankle which had genuinely begun to feel bruised. I'm not quite sure how what happened next, happened, but suddenly I was off balance and she had her arms around me.

'Whoops!' she said. 'You were nearly a gonner, there!'

She released me quickly and I can see now that both of us would have been looking for an excuse to part. As it happened, a train pulled into the station, its destination 'Guildford', displayed on the front.

'My train,' I said, although in different circumstances I'd have been happy to let it go in favour of prolonging the conversation. I turned to take a look at her as the doors closed behind me. She was nowhere to be seen.

I took a seat and began to loosen my shoe. That pedal had taken the skin off my ankle. It was then – as I was easing my shoe off – that I remembered where I had seen her before. It was at my friend Nigel's stag night at the Red Lion in Twickenham. Being a girl she wasn't one of the party, of course, but she'd been in the pub and I'd half-formed the thought of abandoning the lads and trying my luck with her friend or, failing that, with her. But in the nature of these things, by the time I'd had enough to drink, the birds had flown. Well, what a coincidence, I thought. Then I remembered something else: I'd lost my wallet that evening.

Then came another, far more worrying thought. A quick search through my pockets and, true enough, my wallet had gone again! I pulled my shoe off and took out the bracelet I'd lifted from her. It was gold all right, but not a lot of it. I clicked the calculator app on my smartphone. Not too bad: we'd just about broken even.

Kafka's Loo

A public toilet that is locked is worse than no toilet at all. This is what Mandy told the man whose voice came out of the grill when she pressed the button marked, 'Assistance'. He asked her which platform she was on. 'I don't know,' she said, looking about her till she spotted a sign. 'Platform 1.'

'Ah,' said the man, 'that one was closed following repeated misuse.'

'Where can I find one that's open, then?' She wasn't desperate but she'd just had a text from Camille saying she'd missed her train and the next one didn't leave for an hour. Locating a toilet seemed a sensible precaution. The man told her that, regrettably, there was no other on the station. There had once been a toilet on Platform 4 but that had been removed when a lift was installed the previous year. Mandy protested that this was just not good enough. 'So why did you ask me which platform I was on if there was only one loo on the station anyway?' She was trying not to sound hostile. The man conceded that the question may have sounded redundant.

'Although I do like to know where people are,' he explained, 'in case I have to call for assistance.' Mandy enquired, with more sarcasm than was probably wise, what kind of assistance he could offer her right now. He asked her what kind of assistance she needed and after she had told him firmly what should have been obvious, he regretted that it wasn't possible for him to intervene personally, his office being located some miles away. 'I cover a wide area,' he explained. 'You can always use the facilities on the train.'

'But I'm not getting on the train! I'm here to collect someone OFF the train!' Whatever he said in reply was lost on Mandy because at that moment a woman emerged from the toilet. 'Excuse me,' said Mandy, lowering her voice because people were turning to look at her. The woman showed no sign of having heard her and hurried off. 'I've just seen someone come out of the toilet,' complained Mandy into the grill.

'That was probably a cleaner,' suggested the man. The absurdity struck her immediately.

'Why does the toilet need cleaning if it's closed?'

'Because we can't stop the sanitary agency workers using the toilet. They go in to clean and naturally if they need to use the facilities, they will.'

'But if you didn't let them in, the toilets wouldn't get used and then they'd not need cleaning.' Somewhere in the back of her mind Mandy could see that arguing this point was not the direction to be going in. In any case, the logic might prove too much for him. Perhaps it did, or perhaps he had already decided to open up another line of attack.

'Did you say you are not intending to board a train?'

'Yes,' said Mandy. 'I'm here to collect someone.'

'Well then, strictly speaking you are not a customer and toilet facilities are provided solely for customers. Even when they're not provided,' he added, a note of triumph emerging in his voice.

Dangerous as she knew it to be to try and play people like this at their own game, Mandy went for it anyway. She pointed out that she had paid to park her car in the station car park. That made her a customer.

'The car park isn't owned by the railway company,' said the man, clearly sensing victory. 'And don't tell me you bought a sandwich from the kiosk. That's an independent franchise.'

'You haven't read any Kafka by any chance, have you?' The man said that indeed he had. The customer services training manual acknowledged the influence of the great man's work.

Mandy walked back to her car. Frustrated and angry, she sent a text to Camille calling her a stupid cow for missing her train and told her to get a taxi. Then she drove home.

On the Bridge

Once they'd built the bridge over the railway line, linking the two platforms, the whole thing became much easier. Before then you had to cross via a footpath. They closed the gates minutes before the train arrived, which could be frustrating.

You could tell from their body language that most commuters looked forward to Fridays. Even those who weren't spritely enough to run up the steps carried themselves more lightly on a Friday morning. I suppose I was the same when I still had a job to go to. After that, one day was much the same as another; except that Fridays were worse because at the weekend everybody had their freedom, not just me, and they had the money to enjoy it. Free time is great, except when you're broke. Then it becomes boring; boring and depressing, to the point where you start to think the unthinkable, and this is how it seemed to me until one Friday, when the unthinkable became thinkable.

I had this mate, Fred. He and I were of the same mind when it came to the futility of life. He'd been a sporty type, quite unlike me, until a bout of polio had left him with a degree of paralysis. He was still pretty mobile, but he said it had put an end to the squash and a lot else besides. He'd always been reckless, unpredictable and somewhat dark in character, especially after his illness. Thinking about it now, I might even describe him as mad. There were times, though, when he could be quite a joker, and he occasionally made me smile. Briefly.

'We could go together, Pete,' he suggested one day when we were both feeling particularly down. 'Companions to the very end, eh? There's the railway at the end of the road and the bridge'll make it easy.'

Fred brought some rope and tied us together and we climbed onto the balustrade of the bridge, waiting for the non-stop express to be announced. He'd timed it, he said, so we hit the ground at the very moment the train would strike. Death would be instant. There was a light wind and the sun was shining and if it hadn't been for Fred sitting beside me I might have started to have second thoughts. Come to think of it, I was having second thoughts but before I had time to put them into words he gave me a shove and over the edge we went, with no train in sight. Down we plunged with me screaming my head off until there was a horrible jerk and we began to bounce back.

The police were very hard on us. The express had had to be halted and untold disruption to the Friday morning rail service had ensued. I swore I knew nothing about the rope being elastic and I hadn't seen Fred attach a clamp to the railings, but this counted for nothing. Fred couldn't stop laughing and I didn't blame the police at all for cuffing him and bouncing him off a wall.

I didn't speak to him for weeks. I got on with my Community Service Order, which did me the world of good. I do voluntary work now. I might eventually have popped round to see him if it hadn't been for another Friday morning, when he did the same thing again but without me, using rope instead of elastic, tied around his neck and not his waist.

Prelude to an Unknown Story

No doubt there are countless people whose fortunes have been enhanced by the intervention of a Cornish pasty. In this regard, Estelle Luton may not be unusual. What makes her situation different is the fact that she and the pasty that transformed her life never actually met. Neither would 'pasty' have meant anything to her at the time of this proxy-encounter, except that it might have sounded like the French word for a cough drop. She was celebrating her appointment to Head of Human Resources in a pharmaceuticals company in Brive-la-Gaillarde, and her name – not yet anglicised – was Estelle Le Ton.

Meanwhile in Basingstoke, John Anthony Randolph had for some days been concealing an envelope in a secret pocket in his anorak. Inside, probably a little crumpled by then, was a job application he had not mentioned to his boss. If he hadn't found his two colleagues so irritating he might have confided in them.

'Coming for a jar, J.A.R?' they would ask on a Friday evening after work. Being teased about his initials was hardly something to get upset about, he supposed, but did they have to do it *every* Friday? He would have liked to say, 'only if you shut up calling me J.A.R.' but that would have sounded humourless and was not, in any case, guaranteed to make them stop.

Then, one Friday, a week before applications closed, he cleared his desk early, and when the inevitable invitation came, he took it up. At the pub, he tried to get a round in before the others so he'd be able to leave after one drink, but they would have none of it. By the time he managed to drag himself away, he'd had three pints of lager: two of them extra strength. And they were still calling him J.A.R.

He'd intended to tell them about the job application, but when it came to it he realised they'd only poke fun at him. 'Working in Frogland?' he could hear them jeering. What's more, he knew his qualifications weren't really up to it. He had a lower second from a former polytechnic and his French hadn't gone beyond 'A' level. Where had his confidence come from, filling in that form in the first place?

Arriving unsteadily at the station, he was ready to throw the envelope in a bin. The only thing that stopped him was the Cornish pasty kiosk on the platform. He was suddenly famished and a queue was building up. Although he had to wait a few minutes before getting served, he counted himself lucky because at least twenty people had joined the queue behind him. It seemed like the whole of east London had decided to head home at the same time. And then the idea came. When he got to the counter he asked for six large pasties. They cost him three pounds each and at the back of the queue he began selling them for four. People protested but he said, 'better than missing your train isn't it?' and five of them paid up.

He'd only made five pounds, but the discovery that he was capable of such enterprise had him laughing out loud. When his train arrived he squeezed into a seat, and balancing his briefcase on his knees, he took the envelope from his pocket and started to address it. 'Mlle. Estelle Le Ton', he began.

Red Shoes

We'd been waiting half an hour. I'd tried a couple of times to catch the eye of a pretty girl who kept looking up at the arrivals board above my head. Eventually, as she shot a glance at it for the umpteenth time, I thought I might as well say something. I made a remark about these black drivers not wanting to get out of bed in the morning. Maybe it was the wrong thing to say. Maybe she was one of those people who think you're racist if you use the word 'black'. Maybe she thought I was making a pass at her – which I was, I suppose.

She could have smiled, though, couldn't she? Just a little smile, then she could have buried her face in the book she was holding and I'd have got the message. She didn't have to snort. Yes, snort! She shot two jets of smoke out of her nostrils like some small, painted dragon! Then she dropped her cigarette and worked it with her foot like it was my face she was grinding. Maybe I should have told you she was smoking. Everybody smoked in those days.

But do you know what really got to me, standing there watching her foot pulverising that cigarette? It was those shoes: red patent leather with platform soles and heels like cocktail-sticks. A woman hit me with a stiletto-heeled shoe once. I can't remember how it happened. Maybe I'd been drinking. Maybe I'd 'touched her inappropriately', as they say nowadays. I remember watching the blood – my blood – as it dripped onto the bar-room floor.

27

'Civility costs nothing!' I said – to the girl on the platform, I mean. Do you know what she did? She had the bloody nerve to turn her back on me! Well, I don't mind telling you that really made me see red. I reached for her shoulder, just to get her to turn around, that's all, I swear – I barely touched her. But those heels were ridiculous. How can you expect to keep your balance on five-inch heels?

That's when she dropped from sight; just as the train came thundering into the station. She made an awful mess, apparently. I heard later that the shoes were thrown twenty yards and didn't have a mark on them. I didn't ask if the feet were still inside.

Roots

'Hello dear. Can I bend your ear for a mo'? You've got a train to catch? Of course you have. That's why you're here, isn't it? I've never been on one myself but I've seen plenty go by and I can tell you, there's not much I don't know about trains. They're the reason I'm still here and they're the reason – so they keep saying – I've got to go.

Have a seat, there's a good girl – on this bench here: put up ten years ago by a woman whose husband 'loved this place'. I remember him well. He was a bit too 'touchy-feely' for my liking, kept putting his arm around me as he spoke. I could have dropped one on him, but he was a troubled soul and I let him be.

Anyway, you're here to catch a train and it isn't my place to ask 'is your journey really necessary?' They stuck posters up all over the station during the war saying just that. You're too young to remember. It didn't make much difference then and I don't suppose it would make any difference now. I've never understood why people have to be somewhere else other than where they are. Take a look at this lot getting off the train right now: crowds of them, all dragging trolleys. Don't tell me the kids are enjoying this. I've had a few myself over the years but none of them made it. Still, I saw enough being evacuated during the war and believe me I can recognise a miserable kid when I see one. Do this lot want to spend Christmas with their grannies and granddads, their aunts and uncles and the cousins who break their toys but won't let them near any of theirs? Of course they don't. They'd be happier staying at home visiting somebody else's relatives and letting someone else visit theirs. Family life may be a mystery to me, but I've got ears haven't I?

Do you want to know how come I'm still here? Well, we could speculate about that but the simple explanation is that if there wasn't a station here there'd be something else and that something else might have found my presence 'inconvenient'. Just as inconvenient as this new lot are finding me. They need to extend the platform, see, to take the new generation of trains. Half as long again, they are – the only way to cope with increased demand. I can understand that. The trouble is, I'm in the way. So, nothing else for it, I get the chop. Nothing I can do about it. I can't be moved on – not at my age. Roots go too deep, you see.

Well, here comes your train. Thanks for listening. No, don't give me a hug. We don't go a bundle on hugs. Not a lot of people know that. Bye, love.'

The Man in the Red Hat

Inside the café on platform 1, as if steam from the coffee-machine weren't enough, twenty-odd would-be travellers are adding their damp breath to the saturated air. It's freezing outside and so clammy inside, that cases have been put against the door to keep out the cold and stop any more shelter-seekers barging in. It's like being in a sauna. An advertisement engraved on the window that overlooks the platform – written backwards so it's readable from the outside – is vanishing under a patina of condensation. I honestly believe it could start to rain in here at any moment.

The man in the red hat – his name is George but it won't help you to know that – is not waiting for a train. Or, to be more accurate, he is not waiting for a particular train. Any train will do: any train as long as it's fast and as long as it's not stopping. You can see what I'm getting at, can't you?

You wouldn't believe the lengths I've had to go to, to get the idea into his head. *You* might call it murder – I couldn't possibly comment as they say – persuading someone to top themselves. But, honestly, what was I to do, powerless to escape? 'The female of the species is more deadly than the male'? Don't you believe it! Spiders might have it that way but I don't think I could bring myself to inhabit the body of a spider. Whoops! I've let the cat out of the bag now, haven't I? Never mind, let's press on.

Just for a bit of amusement – and God knows there's little of that in my present existence – I decide to get him to write a message in the steam on the window. I start off all

31

wrong, forgetting I have to write backwards, which means I must begin again with less space. 'Help,' I/he writes, 'I am trapped inside the man with the red hat.' The message takes up the entire area of the window pane within his reach. If I wanted to add 'please push this man under a train,' it would mean removing the woman from the table in front, which he is perfectly capable of doing, but I'm not convinced it would be worth the effort on my part. Don't go away with the idea that this sort of malarkey is easy.

Nobody on the outside shows any interest in reading my message, which doesn't really matter; I was only doing it for a lark, life with this bloke being so bloody boring. Five more tedious minutes drag by and then things start to liven up. An automatic announcement is telling customers to stand well back from the platform edge, as the next train to pass through will be the Edinburgh to London non-stop express; in other words: 'Here comes a belter!'

I have done my work well. Clambering over travellers and luggage, he gets himself out of the café and on to the platform. I tell myself I am a clever girl as I begin monitoring his thoughts to see if any of the despair he is feeling needs topping up. But there is a complication. In the struggle to get out of the café, his hat has come off and it's so cold out here it's as though his brain is starting to freeze. He's taken a step beyond the yellow line but he's still a couple of feet from the edge of the platform and all my prompting can't get him to move further forward. It's clear I will have to take the drastic measure reserved for emergencies: I must speak to him directly. This is dangerous because he will actually hear a voice.

I have to confess I am not good at direct communication. I don't get enough practice and when I use it I tend to go over the top. 'Get under that bloody train, you anus!' I scream. George (now the man without the red hat) spins around to confront a man standing behind him, on the other side of the yellow line but only just.

I'd like to describe what happened next but it all happened so quickly and there was no opportunity for me to intervene. I expect you can guess what the upshot was: there was a kafuffle and one of them ended up under the train. It wasn't George.

So here we are, enjoying Her Majesty's hospitality, detained at Her pleasure in an institution for the criminally insane. The staff are very caring and keen to see that he doesn't come to any harm. As you will have gathered, I can't escape from his body until he dies. I am currently working on a plan to get him to Dartmoor, where there are some seriously dangerous people I could get him to insult.

Workers

Marianne has an honours degree in English. It's not from a prestigious university like Oxford or Cambridge. It's not even from York or Reading. But it's still a degree. So what is she doing at the top of a ladder at a London main-line station, with a bucket of paste and a brush, covering the wall with a huge poster? This is a question for others to ask, though most are polite enough not to ask it of Marianne herself. She herself doesn't know the answer any more. She has even forgotten the question.

The posters come rolled in strips. They are numbered, so as long as she follows the sequence correctly she doesn't have to know what the completed work will look like, nor even what the subject matter is. She is no longer curious and will often not be aware of what she has created until she reaches the bottom of the ladder, and only then if she turns to take a look. Usually, she doesn't bother.

Cedric has a degree in mathematics. He is working at the back of a fast-food restaurant on the station concourse, accepting deliveries of hamburgers, breaded fish and chicken wings from a refrigerated lorry. Sometimes he stacks the boxes the wrong way round so you can't read the contents label from the front.

Agnes is cleaning the lavatories. She left school at fifteen, having run away from home. In two years' time, if she keeps up the pace, she will have gained a degree in history from the Open University. She is sometimes told off for singing.

34

Getting Out

I have a perfectly good knowledge of French, but on my regular trips to Brussels I used to make a point of speaking nothing but English. An uneasy cohabitation exists between the French and Flemish-speaking communities and this resonated strongly with my own peculiar circumstances. I was keen to not to be associated with either side.

In the summer I often had lunch in the *Grand Place*, lingering over coffee outside my favourite restaurant with a copy of 'The Daily Mirror'. By my evident ease and choice of newspaper, I hoped not to be taken for a diplomat or a businessman, two roles I once believed I had said goodbye to for good but which an offer a couple of years ago had obliged me to take up again.

That morning, however, there were no English newspapers to be had at the newsagents outside my hotel, so I took a stroll down to the railway station, pretty certain I would find one there. I had no intention of hanging around on the draughty concourse, but the moment I pulled a paper from the rack, a gust of wind caught it and sent the front page tumbling towards the entrance to the platforms. I could have just stuffed the remainder back in the rack and taken another copy – I hadn't yet paid – but the natural orderliness I share with my countrymen sent me scurrying after the flying sheet.

Not surprisingly, given a newspaper's tendency to offer itself up to the wind, the page soon leapt the ticket barrier, and since I had no means of passing through without a ticket, that could easily have been the end of the matter. Instead, it signalled the end of something else entirely.

Just on the other side of the barrier, a woman was standing with her back to me. In due course I learned that she had been on her way to catch a train and been abruptly pulled up by her mobile ringing. Almost immediately, my newspaper had wrapped itself around her shoulders. When I reached the barrier a moment later I found her struggling to extricate herself from it without letting go either of her suitcase or the phone she had in her other hand. I reached across the barrier to take hold of the paper but she somehow sensed the movement behind her and shifted abruptly beyond my reach. As she moved she turned to face me and I recognised her at once.

I was not, strictly speaking, a front-line operative so I had never been given the training required to suppress a display of surprise. I even muttered her name: 'Helga.'

'You must be German,' she said. 'I'm not usually recognised when I'm abroad.' She smiled, evidently happy to be relieved of her anonymity. Then, since I made no attempt to answer, she added, 'or perhaps you just watch German TV?'

I nodded, quite inappropriately since I don't just watch German TV: I *am* German, and I might have said something but we were blocking one of the barriers and evidently causing annoyance. I tried moving aside but jostling travellers weren't making it easy. 'Just like the Belgians,' said the woman playfully, still speaking in German: 'always getting in the way.'

'If that was a reference to our unfortunate past,' I said, 'I can't say I'm amused.'

'My, what a po-face! Lighten up, pal – this is Brussels. The whole place is a joke.' With that she turned and went on her way, finally liberating the front page of that day's 'Daily Mirror', which scampered ahead of her and out of my life.

For the next week I made a point of catching the six o'clock news on German TV. I was disappointed not to see Helga fronting the disasters of the day. Her habit of raising her eyebrows as she announced the next tragic item irritated some Twitterati, although I found the gesture rather endearing, if a little comic. But an unfamiliar, static-eyebrowed face was occupying the screen and a fresh voice tolled the usual litany of global catastrophes. I had – almost – forgotten her, when one morning, just as I was completing my order for breakfast, she came into the hotel dining room and sat down at my table. '*La même pour moi, s'il vous plaît,*' she said to the waiter.

'But you've no idea what I've ordered!' I blurted, so taken aback that I came out with the most inconsequential remark imaginable.

'Since you are passing yourself off as an Englishman it will be something substantial. I only had coffee on the train so whatever it is will be very welcome.' She spread a napkin across her lap and put her elbows on the table. 'Now what language shall we speak?' She raised her eyebrows in that familiar gesture. But like so many of her questions – as I was to learn – she answered it herself. 'English, I think.'

Desperate to regain my balance, I determined not to ask her what all this was about. I told myself that any sign of curiosity on my part would only hand the initiative to her, even though, in reality, I could see she had already seized it. I said nothing and after a moment or two of silence, she nodded her acknowledgement.

'Ok Maurice, if you are not going to ask, I suppose I had better tell you.'

'Only if you really want to . . . Helga.'

'Ah, that's nice. Maurice and Helga. Now we can be friends.'

'I have killed people,' I boasted stupidly, 'who thought they were my friends.' I can't imagine why I said it. I am no James Bond. I just can't help making myself ridiculous when I'm in the company of pretty women.

She threw her head back in a burst of uproarious laughter, seemingly unconcerned by the looks this attracted. 'Don't be silly Maurice! You haven't killed anybody. It would have been in your file.'

'Perhaps you've been looking in the wrong file,' I suggested, sounding even more absurd.

'Born in England in 1949 to a German Jewish mother and unknown father. She had been smuggled out of Germany during the war as a teenager, returning to Bremen in 1952 when she discovered that her parents, whom she had thought dead but who had themselves escaped to Geneva a year after they'd put her on a boat, were alive and well. I could name the primary school you went to . . .' Her voice trailed off. 'Need I go on?' Up went the eyebrows.

Our Full English arrived and neither of us spoke while the waiter poured our coffee. Even when we were alone again, a minute or two passed while we tucked into our sausages, me in the English way, she in the American. Then I said, 'You can get most of that off Google; once you knew who I was. I hadn't realised you'd recognised me at the station.'

'I didn't. My cameraman took a few shots of you.' So there had been a cameraman with her; I hadn't noticed.

'So he had . . .'

'No, he hadn't recognised you either. But you know what cameramen are like – they can't keep their lenses to themselves. Then, merely out of curiosity – not even a hunch – we ran the photos through some software that showed how you might have looked five or ten years ago and found a match on the newsroom photo-base. Easy really.'

I thought, what a bloody cheek, but I didn't say anything. Clicking her tongue at my failure to respond, she picked up my newspaper and made a comment about the unfavourable public reaction to Angela Merkel's immigration policy. Still stunned, not to say unnerved, by her sudden appearance at my table, I mumbled something about Britain's forthcoming referendum on continuing EU membership. Toast arrived with more coffee.

'What I'd really like to know, is what you're up to in Brussels now that requires you to conceal the fact that you're German.'

You've got a bloody nerve, I thought, barging in on me like this, ordering breakfast, helping yourself to my newspaper and telling me what it is "you'd like to know"; yet I couldn't summon up the will to protest.

'The newspaper you mean?' I gestured towards the paper she was still holding. I also lifted an eyebrow but I was no match for her. 'Haven't you noticed,' I said irritably, 'that after all the years, people in countries occupied by the Nazis are still uncomfortable with Germans?'

'Oh come on Maurice, you must be used to that. I certainly am, but you can't go on apologising for something your country did in the past.' Having expressed an opinion, only to see it waved away with a toss of the head, would normally have got me thoroughly rattled, but there was something so entrancing in her wide blue eyes that I was finding it difficult to stay annoyed with her. I was even ready to concede the point.

'You're probably right, Helga, but what gets to me is the fact that, although nothing is said, there is always the "elephant in the room" as the English say. And because we can't mention it, I can't say, "That bloody elephant isn't mine, you know. I'm a Jew!"'

'Oh, I don't know. You could let it out somehow if it's that important to you, couldn't you? Of course you could.' I felt like kicking her.

'And then what would I get? I'll tell you what I'd get: I'd be asked to explain Israel's treatment of the Palestinians. I can't win either way. That's why I pass myself off as English. Why shouldn't I? My father was English, as you have made it your business to find out.' I may have raised my voice a little. 'Anyway,' I went on, leaning towards her, 'I've answered half your question. As

40

for my business, it's nothing special but I'd rather not be talking to the press about it.'

'I'm sure it's all perfectly legal,' she said. 'And morally sound too, no doubt.'

'It's not as though you're a journalist. You just read the news five days a week.'

'Oh, so you think I'm nothing more than a mouth and eyebrows, do you?' She smiled and ran the brows through an exaggerated routine. 'Even worse than that, you haven't noticed that for the last three months I haven't been reading the news at all. I'm a special correspondent now. I have a documentary series in the making.'

That, of course, was an even better reason to keep quiet, but she kept on smiling, chancing her luck that I would at some point give way.

'Ok,' I said, letting my face slip into a resigned half-smile, 'I suppose I ought to feel flattered that a woman twenty years younger than me is pursuing me around town.'

She didn't allow the smile to falter, but the look that came into her eyes was akin to one of an angler who has felt a tug on his line.

'I'm not actually that interested in what it is you're doing, Maurice. I'm not a hard news journalist, if you know what I mean. It's the human dimension that fascinates me: why people do things, where the motivation comes from, what it says about their humanity or lack of it.'

'That all sounds very laudable,' I said, 'and again very flattering if it means you find me interesting for my own sake. But can you study the human being without reference to their work?'

'No, of course not; it's a question of where you place the emphasis – what your ultimate aim is.'

I finished my coffee, folded my napkin on the table and signalled to the waiter to bring the bill for me to sign. I was enjoying her company, but I found her talk of ultimate aims unsettling. It had an uncomfortable historical ring to it. Still, I felt compelled to put the obvious question: 'And what's in it for the subject of your study – in this case, me?'

She chewed her lip for a moment. Surely the question hadn't caught her unprepared. 'Publicity?'

'That's the last thing I need,' I replied, far too quickly, as I immediately realised. I'd been lulled into letting my guard down, even to forgetting that I needed a guard at all. I pushed my chair back awkwardly from the table. 'I'm sorry to be rude,' I said, 'but I've got some phone calls to make. Will you excuse me?' I stood up and held out my hand. 'The breakfast is on the subject.'

'In that case I'll buy us dinner here this evening. 7.30?' Totally flummoxed, I couldn't think of a reply and since I had already let more slip than I'd intended, keeping my mouth shut seemed the soundest option.

Even before I got to my room I was regretting having dealt with her so abruptly. Yes, she was a journalist and yes, she was almost certainly after a story, despite her protestations to the contrary. Yet I was flattered by her attention and, perhaps more importantly, despite a wariness I was struggling not to relinquish, I had begun to like her.

I made a couple of phone calls of little consequence then began to tap out a number I had memorised – some numbers I prefer not to include in my contacts list – when a thought occurred to me. Carrying the phone with me I slipped across to the door and yanked it open. Helga's interest in my affairs evidently did not extend to eavesdropping.

I made the call and then had an hour to wait for a reply. I'd have to stay where I was if I didn't want to risk having to take it in a public place. I ordered some English tea and sat down to figure out what to make of Helga.

As it happened, I didn't meet her for dinner. I left the hotel even before the phone call I'd been waiting for had come through. I left a note for her at reception – I had no other means of contacting her – and headed for the airport.

My mother – well into her nineties – had had a fall at the nursing home two days earlier. No-one had thought it important enough to contact me but some complication had set in and they had now rung to tell me she was dangerously ill with pneumonia.

I arrived at the hospital in the middle of the afternoon. The whole place seemed to be taking a nap and for ten minutes I hurried up and down silent corridors, trying to find someone who knew 'anything about my mother. Eventually, I was directed to reception – the taxi had dropped me by a side door and I had missed the main entrance – only to discover that she had died two hours earlier. Did I want to see her?

Back at the nursing home meals were being served so once again I was reduced to pacing corridors, although this time there were plenty of people about. The difficulty was in finding someone able to give me a second of their time. I wandered into my mother's old room, already a thing of the past. Clearly she had left in a hurry: a wardrobe door hung open and clothes lay on the un-made bed. The air still held the smell of her. I hadn't accepted the hospital's offer to look at her body and I realised now that this smell would be my last memory of her. I opened the door of the bedside cabinet. Inside was a half empty bottle of schnapps – was that the reason for her fall? – and an A5 notepad. I slipped this into my pocket and left.

It wasn't clear who my mother had intended to read the few pages of shaky handwriting she'd left behind in the notepad. Nothing was dated and it was not addressed to anyone. The fact that it was written in Yiddish – a language I have never had any enthusiasm for – left me feeling excluded, as I always had done, from her past.

My father's name was Maurice, it seemed: a married man who eventually left his wife, but only to go off with someone else entirely. This happened around the time my mother discovered her parents were alive and returned to Germany.

A sudden tear dropped onto the page and I found I was crying. I got up from the table and went to the bathroom for some tissues, but after I'd flushed them away I couldn't bring myself to read any more. It felt like an intrusion. Her thoughts were private and she still owned them. The fact that she was dead, at that moment made no difference.

'Even today, I wish my parents had not sent me to England. I would have preferred to stay with them – to die with them if it had come to that. I lost ten years of life I might have shared with them. Neither should I have brought young Maurice to Germany. Better that we should have stayed in England and he not have to face the crisis of identity I know has troubled him.'

Helga passed the sheet of paper back to me. 'Thank you for showing me. I can't read it, of course, but you knew that. What does it say?'

I told her. 'I just needed to show it to someone; to share it somehow.'

'And you showed it to me Maurice, which is lovely. When did she write it?'

'I've no idea. It could have been years ago; it could have been last week.'

'Were you aware of how she felt? Had she ever talked to you about it?'

'No, that's what's so upsetting.'

We were sitting outside a bar in the *Grand Place*, watching a group of school children tumbling out of the City Museum. I could hear French, Flemish, some Arabic as they jostled to be last in the line which two harassed teachers were attempting to form them into. How many of these

45

children had been uprooted on their way to Brussels, I wondered. The thought brought on a feeling of deep melancholy, which I suppose must have shown on my face because Helga, who had been prodding at the slice of lemon floating in her glass of *bière blanche*, suddenly looked up and asked if I would like her to go with me to the funeral. Like a wobbly toy that tips this way and that when you give it a shove, I could never quite keep my balance when I was with Helga.

'That's a ridiculous idea!' I said. 'What the hell would people think?'

'You're obviously something of a loner, Maurice, but there are times when it helps to have someone around. Or are you saying that a gentile wouldn't be welcome?'

'No, of course I'm not saying that, it's just that . . . oh for God's sake what am I saying?'

Helga smiled. 'I don't know what you're saying, Maurice, but whatever it is I'm sorry to have upset you.'

'You haven't upset me.'

'No, of course not. So perhaps, Johnny English, you can tell me why are we suddenly speaking German?'

I put my head in my hands. I would have liked nothing more than to have felt her hand on my arm, but when I eventually looked up she was leaning back in her chair and had lit a cigarette. Was I imagining it, or had her face taken on the expression of an interrogator?

'Who are these people? You said "what would people think?"' Did you mean your family?'

'I don't have any family,' I snapped. 'The Nazis saw to that.'

Helga nodded in the way people do when you mention a personal tragedy. 'No, not my family,' I went on, reverting to English.

'Other people, then? Work colleagues perhaps? People who wouldn't like to see you in the company of a journalist?'

'Am I under arrest? You're supposed to have cautioned me.'

Helga stubbed out her cigarette in the tiny ashtray. 'They obviously don't want customers hanging around long enough to smoke more than one cigarette.' She let out a sigh. 'I don't seem to have got the hang of this journalism lark.'

'Push too hard and you put the punter off?'

'I suppose so. And in any case, it's no way to treat a friend is it – someone who's just shared his mother's last words with you?'

'I don't know why I did that.' She reached across the table and laid her hand on my arm. 'Of course you do.'

The question wasn't raised again and the next day I was at the funeral alone, except for a few of the staff and residents from the care home. There were no tears. In the evening Helga and I had dinner in the old town, during which I made a clumsy attempt at suggesting we sleep together.

'Is my conversation so boring?'

'Oh God, I'm sorry. Is that how I made it sound?'

47

'Just a little. In any case, that's not how I do things. I'm more of a shoe leather and cigarette journalist.'

'You make it sound grubby – hard work but grubby.'

'Not as grubby as shagging my way to a story.'

I flinched.

'Oh Maurice, I'm sorry, there I go again. I keep forgetting what a tender little plant you are.'

'Only when someone gets under my skin.'

She chewed her lip. Where had I seen her doing that before?

'Maybe I will sleep with you.'

If only she had. Or, more accurately, if only we hadn't been delayed by her fancying a Brussels Waffle, and if only the young waiter who brought it to her hadn't recognised me.

As I've said, I was not a front-line operative. Consequently, I never expected to be recognised. Only on one occasion did I slip out of the back room, so to speak, and get involved at operational level. I accompanied a young Lebanese refugee – a boy of thirteen – to Germany. His uncle was a diplomat and should have managed the job himself, but at the last minute he was arrested for a motoring offence in Macedonia. Some clumsy Macedonian cop failed to acknowledge his diplomatic status and we had to get the boy across the border into Germany before a friendly immigration official went off duty. In addition to the child's welfare there was, I recall, a large sum of money at stake.

'*Monsieur Templar,*' he said. '*C'est bon de vous revoir.*' Once more, my lack of training let me down. James Bond would have suggested mistaken identity and slipped a hundred euro note to him in a napkin.

'*Salut, Amal,*' I said.

Getting him to Germany had been his family's idea – for his "own good", of course. He'd been perfectly happy waiting for asylum in Belgium, he told us – Helga now fully engaged in the conversation – so as soon as he was able, he'd made his own way back.

'Sorry to have wasted your time, Monsieur Templar.'

Helga was laughing so much she couldn't sprinkle the sugar over her waffle without covering the table. 'Monsieur Templar! My God, whose idea was that?' When I looked puzzled, she said, 'You must remember Simon Templar, that English detective character.'

I said I'd never heard of him.

'Oh Maurice, you must have done. He was on TV for ages. They kept repeating the series. Roger Moore played the part. Don't you remember? His voice was dubbed by . . .' She clicked her fingers, trying to recall the name. 'I'll remember it in a minute. Anyway, he was called "The Saint" because he did good works.' Then she burst into a fresh peel of laughter. 'That's why, of course! You're helping refugee children. My God, you are "The Saint"!'

I muttered something about her having got her story now.

'Maurice, don't be so ungracious.' She offered me a spoonful of waffle which I refused to accept, until it became clear she was going to hold the spoon out until I did. 'It's quite a story though, you must admit: a man whose mother was smuggled out of Germany during the war and spent the rest of her life regretting it, while her son smuggles children into Germany who then set about smuggling themselves back out again. "The futile tragedy of existence", eh? . . . as somebody said.' She didn't attempt to recall who that might have been.

Helga's novel is coming along nicely, she says. It will be a fictionalised account of my brief career as a child smuggler, now thankfully over. Apparently, she doesn't need me to tell her anything more than she had already learned, preferring instead to have the freedom to make it up as she goes along.

    I moved to Brussels shortly after my encounter with Amal. I see him about the place from time to time, although strangely enough he doesn't acknowledge me now. Helga is working as a documentary film maker in Dresden. She travels around quite a bit, although when she comes to Brussels, which is quite often, it doesn't seem to have anything to do with her work.

55204605R00036

Made in the USA
Charleston, SC
24 April 2016